A Garden for Pig

Written by Kathryn K. Thurman
Illustrated by Lindsay Ward

Kane Miller
A DIVISION OF EDC PUBLISHING

Here is the apple farm, and here is Pig.

For my family
-Kathryn K. Thurman

For my family, and the future Bebop and Rocksteady
-Lindsay Ward

First Edition 2010
Kane Miller, A Division of EDC Publishing

For information contact:
Kane Miller, A Division of EDC Publishing
PO Box 470663
Tulsa, OK 74147-0663
www.kanemiller.com
www.edcpub.com

Library of Congress Control Number: 2009934752

Manufactured by Regent Publishing Services, Hong Kong
Printed May 2010 in ShenZhen, Guangdong, China
1 2 3 4 5 6 7 8 9 10

ISBN: 978-1-935279-24-2

APPLE

Here is Mrs. Pippins,
who owns the farm
and Pig.

Here she is making roasted apples, baked apples, applesauce and apple pie for Pig to eat.

"We grow apples and only apples," says Mrs. Pippins, proudly.

Pig loves life on the farm, but lately something has been troubling him.

n.apple
BORING, SAME
OVER IT!

Pig is tired of apples.
A vegetable would be nice.

Tiptoe, tiptoe. Pig wants a closer look.
He stretches tall.

Creak, goes the fence around the garden.

Crash! Pig tumbles in.

Snap, crack the vines.

Squish, go the squash.

Down they go, seeds and all.

Oh dear. Here comes Mrs. Pippins. She is not happy.
"No more gardening for you." She ties Pig up.

Pig is patient. He'll wait
until Mrs. Pippins leaves.

Stomp, go his feet.

Stretch, goes the rope. Pig pulls hard.

Thud! Pig falls to the ground. The rope will not break.

Oh dear. Here comes Mrs. Pippins. She is not happy.
"No more mischief for you."

Into the pen goes Pig.

Click. The gate closes behind him.

Pig is patient. He'll wait until Mrs. Pippins leaves.

Squeeze. Pig won't fit. He backs up slowly. He charges.

Bam, goes the gate. It will not break.

Oh dear. Here comes Mrs. Pippins. She is carrying something.

Down goes a bowl.

"Time to eat," says Mrs. Pippins. "Apple flambé."

n. apple
flambé
BORING, SAME, OVER IT!

more apples!

Pig digs with his snout. He rolls the dirt over and over. The sun sets.

In the morning, Pig's pen looks a little like a garden.

If only he had some seeds.

"Grumble," says Pig.

"Rumble," goes his tummy.

Ploop! Out come the seeds! Pig had them all along.

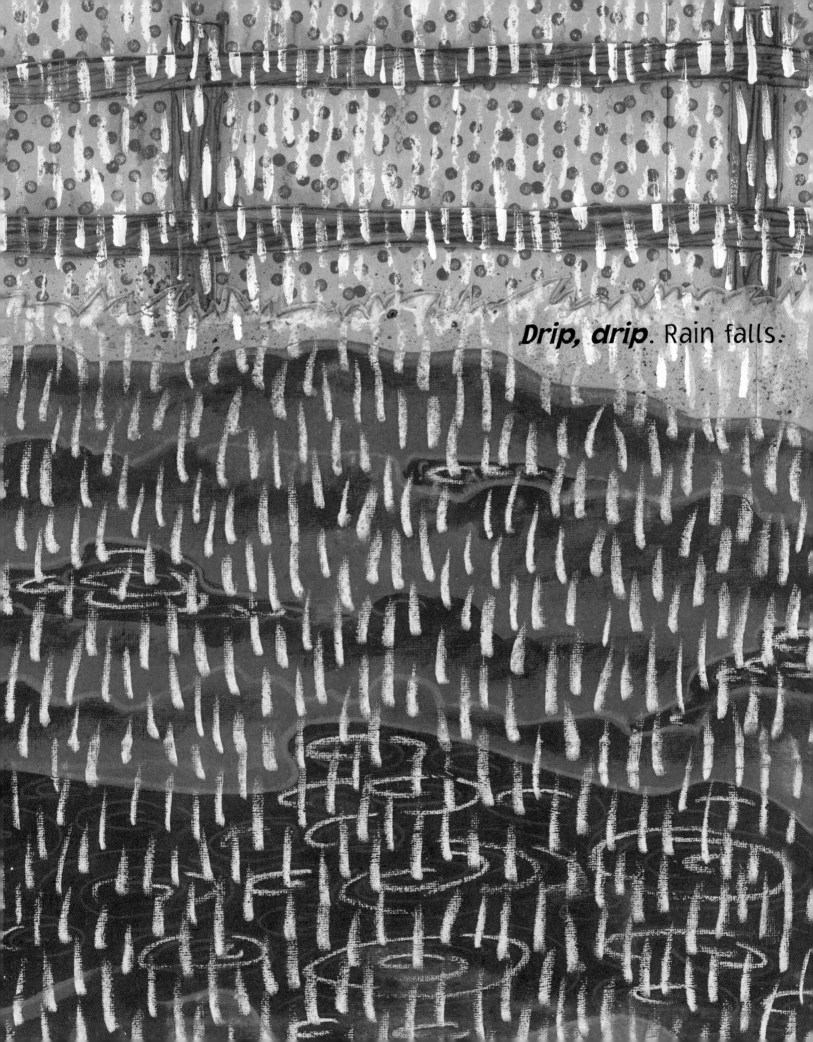

Drip, drip. Rain falls.

And here comes the sun.
Soon the tiny seedlings sprout.

The big leaves unfold.

Yellow flowers bloom.

Squash is growing.

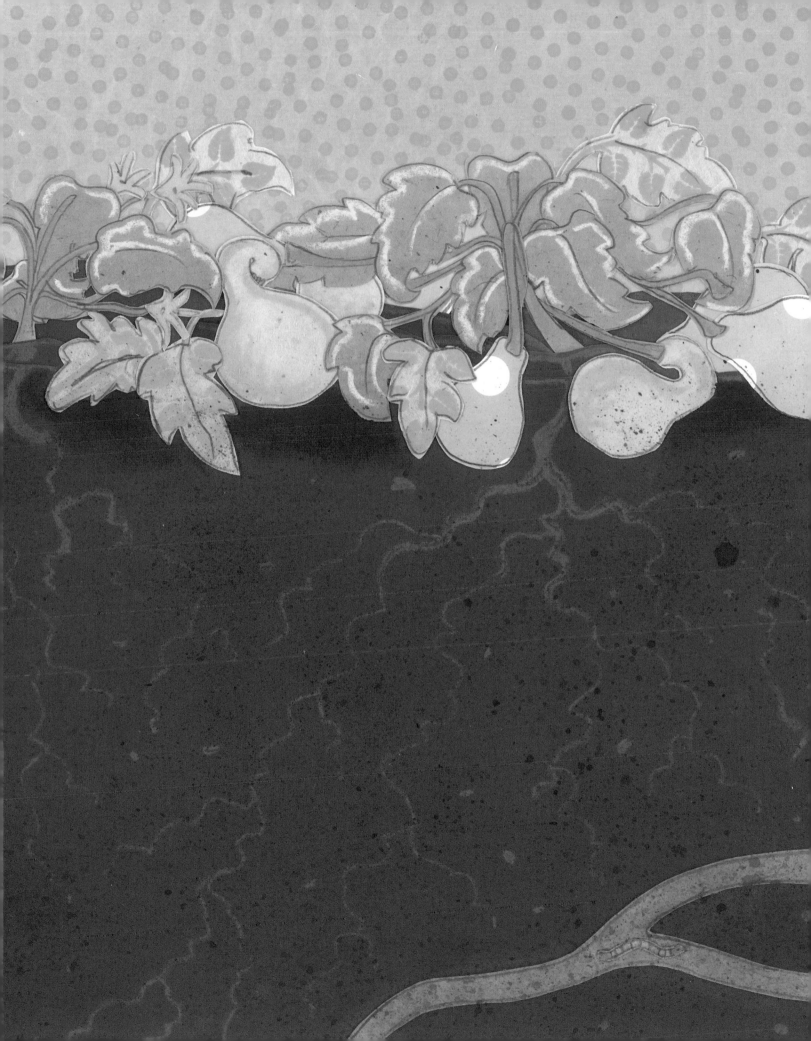

Pig is patient. Soon, large, ripe squash fill his pen. Pig is very busy.

Smoosh, go the squash

Down go the seeds, and ***gulp***, Pig is happy.

Pig's Tips for Growing Your Own Organic Garden

with help from Kathryn K. Thurman

In 2003, our family's pet pig really did plant his own organic squash garden. The squash were big and grew like crazy. They were organic, because no pesticides or manmade fertilizers were used. Pesticides are chemicals, which kill bugs that might eat or damage plants. But not all bugs are bad. Some are great helpers! By understanding how plants and animals work together in nature, you can have a garden full of your own favorite fruits and vegetables. Best of all, you will know that everything in your garden is safe for you to eat and was grown in harmony with all living things.

Plant the Garden

Step 1: *Pick a sunny location and start small.* Remember, even small gardens can be a lot of work. The more space there is, the more weeds there will be to pull. Make sure your location gets sun and is easy to water.

Step 2: *Pick quick growing seeds.* Like Pig, you will need patience. Luckily, some varieties of plants sprout quickly. Radishes, lettuce, peas, and bush beans are just a few of the varieties that won't keep you waiting too long.

Step 3: *Plant your seeds at the right time.* Some plants like to be started earlier than others. It will say on the back of the seed package when to plant. Also, don't worry about planting in straight rows, Pig didn't. Why not plant your seeds in a fun shape? How about in the shape of a pig?

Keep Weeds and Pests Away the Natural Way

Mulch to keep weeds away. Add a thick layer of pine needles, wood chips, leaves, or straw to the top of the soil. Mulch works by smothering weeds and keeping sunlight away from them. It also adds nutrients to the soil.

Welcome the Ladybugs and get rid of the aphids. Aphids damage plants by sucking the juice out of them and spreading disease. Ladybugs will eat over 5,000 aphid bugs in their one-year lifetime.

Use companion plants. By planting certain plants next to one another, you can repel insects, provide shade and attract the good bugs. Here are a few vegetables that do well together. Lettuce does great with carrots, radishes and cucumbers. Squash does well with corn and marigold flowers.

Build a fence. A fence will help keep away deer, rabbits and other creatures that might find your garden irresistible.

Fertilize with Compost and Let the Worms Help You

Healthy plants start with great soil and compost. Composting happens all around us. After leaves fall from the trees or old grass clippings sit for a long time, they eventually turn into dark, earthy-smelling dirt called, "compost." Packed with nutrients, compost helps to make plants strong, healthy, and disease resistant.

Leave it to the worms. There are possibly no creatures that are better helpers than these slippery friends. They eat more than half their own body weight of old leaves and plant material! The castings they leave behind are great compost. Worms also dig tunnels, which allow air and water to soak into the soil. Fungi, bacteria and other insects, like sow bugs and centipedes, also help with composting.

Making Your Own Compost Bin – A Recipe for Success

You can buy compost or you can make it yourself. There are several ways to make a compost bin, but here is a simple way to turn an ordinary outdoor garbage can into a compost bin.

1. Punch several holes into the bottom of a garbage can.
2. To the can, add a layer of kitchen scraps like fruit and vegetable peelings, coffee grounds, eggshells, and nutshells. Never add meat, bones, fish or grease. They will slow down the composting process.
3. Now, add a layer of natural material. This can be small twigs, bark, shredded paper, sawdust, wood chips, manure, hay, weeds and other garden waste.
4. Sprinkle each layer with some water.
5. Every ten days, roll the can on its side to mix the mixture. You can add more plant material at any time.
6. Harvest the compost in two months and watch your plants thrive.

Pick and munch! Pig will agree, there is nothing better than eating something you grew yourself. ***Gulp***